Palace Pets

Meet

Treasure & Bayou

written by Amy Sky Koster
illustrated by the Disney Storybook Art Team

DISNEP PRESS

New York • Los Angeles

For information address Disney Press,
1101 Flower Street, Glendale, California 91201.

ISBN 978-1-4847-2298-5
F383-2370-2-14251
Printed in China
First Edition
1 3 5 7 9 10 8 6 4 2

For more Disney Press fun, visit www.disneybooks.com

A Kitten Named
Treasure

Treasure loved the beach. Every day she'd play in the rolling waves and dream of adventure.

Most cats are afraid of water. But not Treasure!
Treasure was sweet and brave and playful.
But most of all, Treasure was a very curious cat!
One day Treasure got curious about the sea,
so she stowed away on a ship.

Little did Treasure know that she was on
Prince Eric's ship! Imagine the royal crew's surprise
when they discovered a furry little stowaway.

Treasure was just
as surprised—and worried.

Would she have
to scrub the deck?

Would they make her
walk the plank?

No! Prince Eric wanted to adopt Treasure.

The curious kitten with the shiny red hair reminded him

of someone he loved very much . . . Princess Ariel.

When the ship returned to port, Prince Eric presented the kitten to his bride. Ariel cuddled Treasure close. The little kitten purred softly in the princess's arms.

Treasure is now Ariel's little treasure, and they collect trinkets and swim together all day long.

A Pony Named
Bayou

Bayou lived in the tiny country of
Maldonia, but she was moving to a big city.
Prince Naveen's parents were taking her to
live with Princess Tiana.

Bayou boarded a ship and set sail for America. After a long
ocean voyage, Bayou finally met the princess at the
Port of New Orleans. Tiana had a surprise for her.

A costume! Bayou had arrived on
Fat Tuesday, just in time for the Mardi Gras
parade, a New Orleans tradition.

But Bayou wasn't used to costumes, and she missed her home in Maldonia. Luckily, Tiana had just the thing to make her feel better: a slice of apple pie Tiana had baked herself.

As Bayou gobbled up the pie, she heard the parade music begin. The little horse was still scared, but now she was curious, too. With Tiana by her side, Bayou went to watch the parade.

It was amazing!

The next day, Tiana introduced Bayou to her best friend, Charlotte LaBouff. Bayou would be living in the cozy stables at the LaBouffs' estate.

Then Tiana took Bayou to her
world-class restaurant. Bayou gazed at
Tiana's Palace. She knew she had
found a new home.